Dear mous
Welcome to the world of

Geronimo Stilton

MINI MYSTERY

4

THE RODENT'S GAZETTE
EDITORIAL STAFF

Geronimo Stilton
A learned and brainy mouse; editor of *The Rodent's Gazette*

Thea Stilton
Geronimo's sister and special correspondent at *The Rodent's Gazette*

Trap Stilton
An awful joker; Geronimo's cousin and owner of the store Cheap Junk for Less

Benjamin Stilton
A sweet and loving nine-year-old mouse; Geronimo's favorite nephew

Geronimo Stilton

THE CAT GANG

Scholastic Inc.

ISBN 978-0-545-64288-0

Based on an original idea by Elisabetta Dami.
www.geronimostilton.com

Published by Scholastic Inc., 557 Broadway, New York, NY 10012.
SCHOLASTIC and associated logos are trademarks and/or registered trademarks of Scholastic Inc.

Text by Geronimo Stilton
Original title Le banda del gatto
Cover by Giuseppe Ferrario and Giulia Zaffaroni
Illustrations by Valeria Brambilla (pencils and inks)
and Mirko Babboni (color)
Graphics by Michela Battaglin and Marta Lorini

Special thanks to Kathryn Cristaldi
Translated by Andrea Schaffer
Interior design by Becky James

Fingerprint on cover and page i © NREY/Shutterstock

First printing, January 2014 by Scholastic Malaysia, operating under Grolier (Malaysia) Sdn. Bhd.

Printed in Malaysia

BILLS, BILLS, AND MORE BILLS!

It was a bright **Fall** day. It was the kind of day that makes a mouse want to stop **scampering** and just breathe.

From the window of my office, I stared out at the **colorful** leaves and sniffed the crisp air. Ah . . .

If only I could shut out the sounds of the bustling **newsroom** behind me. What newsroom? Oh, excuse me! I haven't introduced myself. My name is Stilton, *Geronimo Stilton*, and I run *The Rodent's Gazette*, the most famouse newspaper on Mouse Island.

Dwayne Digitpaws, the financial manager, began squeaking in my ear.

"Mr. Stilton! We need to go over the monthly **bills**!" he insisted.

Bills, bills, and more bills! If there's one thing I can't stand, it's dealing with the monthly **bills**.

I tried to convince Dwayne to talk to me after lunch, but it was as if his ears were **stuffed** with cheese. He kept on squeaking.

"**LOOK** here, Mr. Stilton," he said. "This month's phone bill is **$4,500**! And the cost of paper is ridiculous! We spent **$30,000**! And the new photocopier cost **$7,000**!"

$4,500!

SIGH!

$30,000!

$7,000!

There was no way to stop him. So I spent the whole morning going over the numbers and paying bills.

So much for my relaxing **Fall** morning.

Finally, Dwayne told me I needed to sign some documents over at the **BANK**.

"No problem," I agreed, heading for the door. I decided I would stop at home for lunch first. At least it would be peaceful there.

But I was **wrong**. . . .

SMILE, MR. STILTON!

As soon as I left *The Rodent's Gazette*,
someone blinded me with a flash, yelling,
"Nice shot, Mr. Stilton!"

I recognized him immediately. "Aren't
you **Red Paparatz**, the photographer
for the famouse, scandalous newspaper
Chatter?" I asked.

"Exactly, Mr. Stilton!" answered Red, SNAPPING another picture. "Smile!"

I scratched my head. "Um, why are you taking my photo?" I mumbled as I was blinded by another series of flashes.

"I'm photographing you because I want to work for you!" replied Red. "I'll show you how good I am. Smile, please!"

By now I was starting to see STARS from all that flashing light.

"Please stop!" I wailed.

But Red kept snapping away.

FLASH!
FLASH!

"I'll stop when you hire me to work for your newspaper!" he demanded.

Luckily, I had just arrived in front of my house. "Ahem, I — I — I need to think about it, **Red**," I stammered. "I'll let you know as soon as I can."

Then I flung open the door and raced inside.

I was safe at last!

FLASH! FLASH!

To recover from my stressful morning, I treated myself to a delicious lunch of macaroni and cheese, mozzarella rolls, and **chocolate**-covered cheddar logs.

After lunch, I lay down for a quick mouse nap. I was awakened by the

sound of the telephone **ringing**.

It was Dwayne Digitpaws.

"Mr. Stilton!" he shrieked. "What are you still doing at home? The bank closes in fifteen minutes!"

Cheese niblets! I had forgotten all about going to the bank!

I left right away, but just outside my door stood an annoying surprise: Red Paparatz with his **flashing** camera!

"So, Mr. Stilton, will you hire me?" he asked as he followed me.

"Not now, Red," I muttered, racing along. "I'm in a *hurry*. I have to get to the bank."

But that didn't stop Red.

"Perfect!" he squeaked. "I can take some *ACTION* shots of you!"

I was running so fast, I was almost hit by a black van. It roared past me and **screeched** to a stop in front of the bank.

Meanwhile, **Red Paparatz** was clicking away.

FLASH! FLASH! FLASH!

FOUR MYSTERIOUS MICE

Four rodents wearing **dark** raincoats and **serious** expressions climbed out of the van. They headed into the bank.

But when I tried to follow them inside a moment later, the door was **locked**!

"**Sour Swiss rolls!**" I exclaimed. How strange! Those rodents had scampered inside just ahead of me.

Oh, well. At least **Red Paparatz** had stopped taking my picture and was taking shots of the bank instead.

Quiet as a mouse, I snuck back home. When I arrived, the phone rang. It was my sister, Thea.

"There was a robbery at the Bank of New Mouse City!" she said. "I'll meet you at the office!"

Rancid rat poison!

"But I was just there a half hour ago!" I cried.

I hung up the phone and **turned** on the TV. A newscaster was interviewing a **bank teller**.

"Did you see how many there were?" she asked.

"There were four, all dressed in **BLACK**," replied the teller. "Then an **ENORMOUSE** cat appeared."

"A cat?" asked the newscaster. "Are you sure?"

"Absolutely!" the teller replied. "It was the most **frightening** cat I've ever seen!"

I shuddered. An enormous cat was **TERRORIZING** the rodents of New Mouse City! I was scared out of my **fur**, but I needed to get the story for the paper. If only we had pictures. Then I remembered **Red Paparatz**. He had photographed everything! I had to find him!

I'M INTO CLOSE-UPS

I opened my front door to search for Red Paparatz and was **blinded** by a **FLASH**! He had found me! We went to the newsroom together and Red downloaded more than two hundred photos onto Thea's **computer**. Too bad they were all terrible.

"Do you like my style, Mr. Stilton?" Red asked. "I'm into CL◎SE-UPS."

I tried not to cry. There were shots of my nose, my paw, and my whiskers. Finally, an **image** appeared on the screen. It showed all FOUR VILLAINS putting the money into the van.

"How **strange**," commented Thea. "Someone is missing. It doesn't add up. . . ."

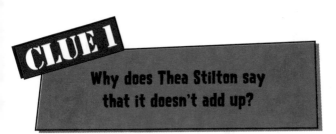

CLUE 1

Why does Thea Stilton say that it doesn't add up?

Oops!

The following **morning**, I woke to the sound of the phone ringing.

"Hello?" I squeaked.

It was **Dwayne Digitpaws**.

"Did you go to the bank?" he asked.

Oops! I forgot again!

"I'm on my way to the **BANK OF NEW MOUSE CITY** right now!"

Hello?

"Not that bank, Mr. Stilton!" he said with a sigh. "The papers are at the

Rodent Savings Bank!"

What?! I had gone to the **wrong** bank the previous day.

I threw on my clothes . . .

. . . gulped down my breakfast . . .

. . . and raced for the door . . .

. . . when the doorbell rang.

It was my nephew **BENJAMiN** and his friend **Bugsy Wugsy**.

"Hi, Uncle Geronimo!" my nephew squeaked. "Guess what? It's a school **holiday**. Can we hang out with you?"

I gave Benjamin a huge **hug**. Oh, how I **love** that little mouse!

"Of course, my dear nephew," I said. "But first we need to take a quick trip to the bank. Then we'll go to my office. Sound good?"

"**Yes!**" Benjamin and Bugsy exclaimed.

A few minutes later we reached the bank. I couldn't believe my eyes.

CLUE 2

Look at the illustration on the next page. What does Geronimo see that is so surprising?

THE BLACK VAN . . .
AGAIN!

Sour Swiss rolls! The black van that I had seen yesterday was parked in front of the bank . . . again!

I turned as WHITE as a slice of mozzarella.

A minute later, a **bright** flash blinded me. Can you guess who was taking my picture?

It was **Red Paparatz**, of course! "Not today, Red . . ." I began to tell him. Then suddenly, four rodents dressed in **BLACK** sprang from the van.

Red tried to take a picture, but the smallest rodent **SWIPED** the camera. Then we were all shoved into the bank.

I gulped. Something told me these rodents were up to **no good**!

THE ONE, THE ONLY, THE INCREDIBLE CAT-CAT!

As soon as we were inside, the biggest rodent immediately disconnected the bank surveillance camera.

"Hello, everyone!" the smallest rodent

squeaked. "I'd like you all to meet the one, the only, the incredible **Cat-Cat**!"

An **enormouse** cat appeared right before our eyes.

WHAT A SCARY FELINE!

Meet Cat-Cat!

"Cat-Cat will obey all my orders," the smallest rodent, who seemed to be

the leader, continued. "I'd advise you to do as I say if you don't want to become cat **kibble**!"

Benjamin squeezed my paw tightly in fear. I tried not to scream. **Holey cheese**, that little mouse has some **grip**!

Meanwhile, the smallest rodent had turned to the bank manager, **Martin Moneywhiskers**.

"Open the safe, Moneybags," the robber demanded.

"It's Moneywhiskers," grumbled the manager. He led the robbers to the safe. The giant cat followed, claws **screeching** against the marble floor.

Ugh! How I hated that sound! It reminded me of **PAWNAILS** on a chalkboard. Cat-Cat really needed to find himself a giant nail file or a cat salon.

I was so busy thinking about nails, I didn't see Moneywhiskers hit a **RED** button on the wall. Within seconds, **STEEL** bars shot up from the floor.

The bars created a barrier between the robbers and the rest of us.

What a fabumouse antitheft system!

Forget the Fish Sandwich!

Everyone cheered. Well, except for the bank robbers. The gang kept **piling** money from the safe into laundry sacks. And then the **strangest** thing happened. . . .

The leader of the robbers ordered Cat-Cat to **advance**. And to our amazement, he did!

Cat-Cat walked through the STEEL bars as if they were invisible!

He towered over Moneywhiskers with his teeth bared.

Oh, what a **fur-raising sight**!

"Your tricks won't work with us, Moneybags!" the little robber squeaked. "Now, if you hit any more buttons, I'm going to tell Cat-Cat to forget the fish sandwich he packed for lunch and EAT you instead! It's up to you!"

The manager held up his paws in defeat.

Then the four robbers left the bank with the money, and the big cat disappeared into thin air, exactly as he had appeared.

It was strange.

Very Strange.

I'd like to **FILL** you in on what **happened** next, but I can't. That's because as soon as the **ROBBERS** left, I *fainted!*

ANOTHER BIG SCOOP!

When I opened my eyes, I found myself in my office.

"Wake up, Uncle Geronimo!" said my nephew Benjamin. "You're okay."

"Quit NAPPING, Gerry Berry," said my sister, Thea. "We've got a story to work on!"

"Check out the photo I took, Mr. Stilton!" That was Red Paparatz.

Photo?

I bolted upright.

"How did you get a picture without your camera?" I asked Red.

"Resourcefulness, Mr. Stilton!" he replied. "I carry a digital **micro-camera** in my hair at all times!"

Red showed me the images.

"But these are pictures of the CEILING and the inside of your ear," I observed.

"Oops," said Red, snatching back the photos and **FLIPPING** through them. "Here it is!"

He held up a **blurry** photo. It showed the back of the giant cat.

"Can we publish it?" Red squeaked.

The next day, the **photo** was on the front page of *The Rodent's Gazette*. The paper sold like freshly baked cheese Danish at **The Pastry Rat**.

"There's something strange about that photo," Benjamin said. "Look at the **cat**!"

Look at the cat!

"Of course, Uncle G!"

exclaimed Bugsy. "Look at the cat!"

"Right, the **cat**," I mumbled, though I had no idea what they were **squeaking** about.

Of course, Uncle G!

CLUE 3

Do you notice something strange about the cat in Red Paparatz's photo?

G-G-G-Good Kitty!

"If there's no **shadow** . . ." said Bugsy.

". . . and it's TRANSPARENT . . ." added Benjamin.

". . . the only possible conclusion . . ." added Thea.

". . . is that the cat is a **g~g~ghost**!" I stammered, feeling faint again.

BENJAMIN giggled. "No, Uncle, the conclusion is that the cat is a **FAKE**!"

"Now we just have to figure out how the **ROBBERS** make the cat appear," Bugsy said.

"A **FAKE**, of course." I **coughed**, pretending I knew what that meant. Lucky for me, I wasn't in the **dark** for long.

Benjamin suggested we ask my old friend **Professor Paws Von Volt** for help.

Professor von Volt is a brilliant scientist and inventor. We headed to his **laboratory**.

"Ah, yes," squeaked the professor after he had examined the photo. "There is no doubt that this is a **hologram**. It's a three-dimensional image that is projected and seems to be real."

He turned off the **LIGHT** and turned on something that looked like an old film projector. A second later an **AMAZING** tropical rain forest appeared all around us!

Then we heard the most terrifying **ROAR**. Frozen in horror, I watched

as a ferocious **TIGER** materialized before us.

"G-g-g-good kitty," I squeaked, trembling with fear.

Suddenly, Benjamin and Bugsy began walking toward the beast with strange smiles on their snouts.

"**Noooooo!**" I yelled, jumping in front of them to protect them.

But then the **weirdest** thing happened.

The tiger opened its jaws and . . . I passed through them without even a **SCRATCH**.

The professor turned on the light. "What did I tell you?" he said. "Some

ROOOOOOAAAAAAR!!!

holograms are so good, they seem as real as that tiger," he explained.

Benjamin hugged me. "You were very COURAGEOUS, Uncle Geronimo," he squeaked.

"Yep, we sure wouldn't want to get eaten by a hologram, Uncle G," Bugsy teased.

I coughed. Oh, how embarrassing!

Professor von Volt explained that in order to make a hologram, the projector-like machine has to be close by. Otherwise, the image will be blurred.

"So the robbers had to set up a projector somewhere near the bank," Thea reasoned.

"And I know just how they did it!" Benjamin **EXCLAIMED** suddenly.

"Me, too!" Bugsy and Thea shouted in unison.

Even Red Paparatz chimed in.

"Of course, it's so **OBVIOUS**!" he agreed.

"Obvious, right," I added, completely clueless. Why, oh, why was I always the last one to FIGURE things out?

Later that night, I called Benjamin and he explained everything to me.

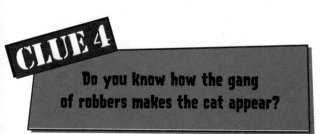

CLUE 4

Do you know how the gang of robbers makes the cat appear?

A Large, Heavy-Duty Net

Over the next week, the Cat Gang continued to rob the banks of New Mouse City.

The **ROBBERS** followed the same routine every time. They parked their van in front of the bank.

Then they **ROBBED** the bank. When it was time to leave, they made Cat-Cat (or the hologram of Cat-Cat) chase everyone away. After that, the robbers were free to drive off with the stolen **loot**.

Even though I published an article in *The Rodent's Gazette* about the **FAKE** cat, with an interview from Professor von Volt, no one in New Mouse City believed me.

Even the mayor, **Frederick Fuzzypaws**, insisted that the **terrifying** Cat-Cat was as real as whiskers on a **mouse**. He told everyone not to worry because the police had a plan.

"The police have constructed a large, heavy-duty **NET**," Mayor Fuzzypaws explained. "When I give the word, they will throw the net over the giant cat and catch him!"

Of course, the plan didn't work. The giant cat walked right through the net without blinking an eye. The police went home **discouraged** and empty-pawed, and the robbers continued to steal from more banks.

Finally, I had to do something about the situation. My dear nephew must have been thinking the same thing, because later that day he called me.

"**I have an idea**," he said.

Don't Worry, Uncle Geronimo

We **all** met at my house.

Of course, this included my sister, Thea, Benjamin, Bugsy Wugsy, and Red Paparatz, who by now was part of the TEAM.

We sat around the table, talking. I tried my best to concentrate but my mind kept wandering. I had bought some **cheesy donuts** at the Stop and Squeak, and I couldn't take my eyes off them. Would it be rude to be the first to start **munching**? I was still *drooling* over the donuts when Benjamin began to squeak.

"We know the giant cat isn't real," Benjamin explained. "It's a hologram. But the thieves don't know we know their **SECRET**. So all we have to do is **SURPRISE** them!"

Suddenly, I wasn't thinking about donuts anymore.

"S-s-s-surprise them?" I stammered. Did I mention how much I hate **SURPRISES**?

"Don't worry, Uncle Geronimo," Benjamin replied, giving me a kiss. "We'll be okay."

I **melted**. How could I say no to my **sweet** nephew?

SUBTRACT, DON'T ADD!

Benjamin took out a map.

"I marked all of the banks in the city on this map," he explained. "There are **TEN** altogether. So far the thieves have broken into **FIVE** of those banks —"

"That means there are **FIFTEEN** banks left!" Red Paparatz interrupted. "I'm good with math."

Bugsy **ROLLED** her eyes. "You need to subtract, not add," she corrected him. "There were ten banks and they already robbed five. That means there are **FIVE** left!"

"I knew that," Red said, turning as **red** as his hair. "Ten minus five equals **FIVE**. Any mouselet knows that one."

$$10-5=5$$

"Anyway," Benjamin continued. "There are five banks left to watch. So I drew a line from all the banks that have been robbed to all the ones left. The outline formed a **SHAPE**. Can you tell what it is?"

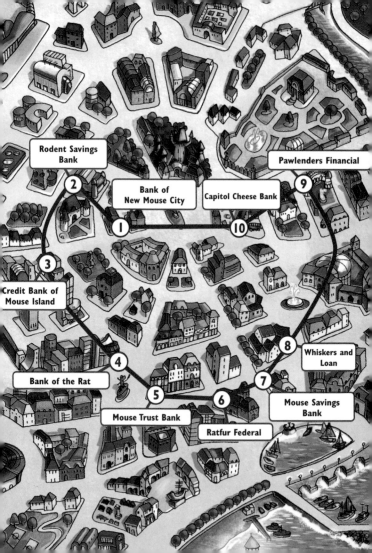

Rodent Savings
Bank

Pawlenders Financial

Bank of
New Mouse City

Capitol Cheese Bank

Credit Bank of
Mouse Island

Whiskers and
Loan

Bank of the Rat

Mouse Savings
Bank

Mouse Trust Bank

Ratfur Federal

BENJAMIN'S PLAN

Benjamin spread the map on the table and we all stared at it.

"It's the face of a **cat**!" Red Paparatz shouted. "I'm good with **PICTURES**."

This time, he was right.

"Exactly!" Benjamin agreed. "The cat is the **symbol** of the gang of robbers."

"So if the thieves are going to finish the cat **DESIGN**, then we just have to figure out which bank they will hit next," Bugsy added.

I shivered. This plan was getting more **fur-raising** by the minute!

Oh, what a rodent's nightmare!

Then, just when I thought things couldn't get any **SCARIER**, they did.

"**AUNT THEA**, can you and Uncle Geronimo please follow the robbers' van with your **motorcycle**?" Benjamin asked *sweetly*.

My daredevil sister, Thea, was happy to help.

"When do we leave?" she squeaked **excitedly**.

I felt faint. Forget the Cat Gang! Riding on Thea's **motorcycle** was way more terrifying!

"I think I'm g-g-g-getting **SICK**," I stammered. "M-m-m-maybe I should stay behind."

But no one was listening.

"After you spot the van, Bugsy and I, along with **Professor von Volt**, will take action," Benjamin was saying.

Professor von Volt was coming? I started to ask Benjamin if the professor could take my place on Thea's motorcycle, but Thea interrupted.

"There's only one **Problem** with your plan, Benjamin," my sister said. "You see, even **if** we are able to find the Cat Gang's van, and **if** we are able to figure out which bank they will strike next, we will have no idea **when** they will strike."

Benjamin grinned. "That would be true, Aunt Thea, if Bugsy hadn't checked the days and the hours of the robberies. She **discovered** they follow a pattern."

	Bank	Day	Time
Robbery #1	Bank of New Mouse City	Monday 15	3 p.m.
Robbery #2	Rodent Savings Bank	Tuesday 16	4 p.m.
Robbery #3	Credit Bank of Mouse Island	Wednesday 17	5 p.m.
Robbery #4	Bank of the Rat	Monday 22	3 p.m.
Robbery #5	Mouse Trust Bank	Tuesday 23	4 p.m.
Robbery #6	Ratfur Federal or Capitol Cheese Bank	?	?

Bugsy showed us a chart she had made of all of the robberies. It listed the names of the banks robbed and the **DATE** and **time** of each robbery.

I stared at the chart closely.

Holey cheese! There was a pattern!

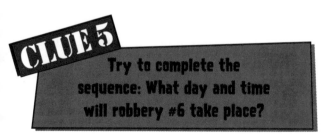

CLUE 5

Try to complete the sequence: What day and time will robbery #6 take place?

KEEP YOUR EYES OPEN!

The next robbery would be on Wednesday the twenty-fourth at **5 P.M.** And so at **4:45 P.M.** on Wednesday, we put *Operation Catch the Cat Gang* in motion.

Benjamin, Bugsy, and Red Paparatz stayed with Professor von Volt while Thea and I got on her motorcycle.

"Ready, **Gerry Berry**?" my sister asked, **revving** the engine.

I was ready all right. Ready to **JUMP** off that scary motorcycle, run home, and **hide** under the covers! But what could I do?

"Sure," I muttered, holding on for dear life! Oh, how I hate **motorcycles**! With a roar, the bike **ZIGZAGGED** through the streets of the city. Even though I know Thea is a skilled driver, I kept my eyes **closed** the whole time.

It took us ten minutes to complete the run between Ratfur Federal and **Capitol Cheese Bank**. But when we reached the place where we had started, we still hadn't spotted the van. And it was 5 p.m. exactly!

"We're going to have to do that again," Thea declared. "And this time, try keeping your eyes OPEN, Gerrykins!"

Ooops! Maybe that's why I hadn't spotted the van!

We took off again at an **alarming** speed. I was scared squeakless! Still, I practiced taking some deep *breaths* and forced myself to remain calm. It worked! Just then, I spotted the van!

Do you also see the
Cat Gang's van?

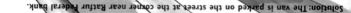
Solution: The van is parked on the street at the corner near Ratfur Federal bank.

Meeeooowww!

Thea called Professor von Volt and the others to let them know we had found the van. Then we went back to the front of the bank.

I could hardly believe my eyes. The VAN was there, parked on a side street. And judging by the beam of light that came from the side facing the bank, they were already projecting the cat inside the building!

Before long, Professor von Volt arrived with Benjamin, Red, and Bugsy. The professor was also driving a van, which he parked in front of the bank.

I was a **nervous** wreck, but the professor was **relaxed**.

"Let's wait until they finish the **ROBBERY**," he said with a chuckle.

How could the professor remain so **calm**? By now my **fur** was standing on end!

A few minutes later, the door to the bank **FLEW** open and the four robbers strode out. They were followed by the terrifying **Cat-Cat**.

Even though I knew he wasn't real, my heart began to pound like crazy.

"Remain calm!" the professor yelled to passersby. "It's only an optical **illusion**!"

Still, everyone near the bank took off and, I'm embarrassed to say, I hid behind Red Paparatz and his **camera**.

"Give up now!" Professor von Volt yelled at the robber rats. "We know that cat isn't **real**!"

The leader just glared at us.

"Oh yeah?" he smirked. "Is this REAL enough for you?"

Just then the **cat** let out a bloodcurdling meow that sent shivers down my spine.

"MEEEOOOWWW!"

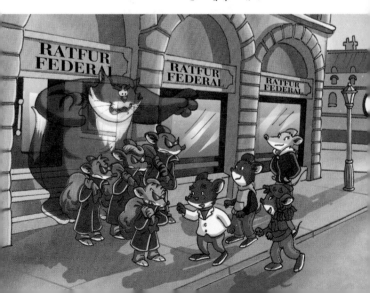

Professor von Volt smiled.

"Not bad for a **kitty**," he commented.

"But we brought a **real** cat."

All of a sudden, a **TIGER** twice the size of Cat-Cat appeared. The tiger opened its massive jaws and **ROARED**.

The Cat Gang took off with their **tails** between their legs. What a sight!

Even I had to laugh. Of course, I knew our tiger was **fake**. The first time I had met him was in Professor von Volt's lab!

THE CAT GANG IS CAPTURED!

The next day, Red Paparatz's photos were all over the front page of *The Rodent's Gazette*. **CAT GANG CAPTURED!** the headline declared. The **PAPERS** practically **flew** off the shelves.

I was so happy. The bad guys were behind bars, and I could finally relax in my cozy mousehole and enjoy the beautiful **autumn** leaves . . . or maybe the **spring** flowers . . . or the **wintry** snow-capped mountains . . . **That's right!** I can enjoy all four seasons at once if I want to. How?

Geronimo Stilton, Publisher
www.geronimostilton.com

17 Swiss Cheese Center
New Mouse City

The Rodent's Gazette

CAT GANG CAPTURED!

It's easy! After we captured the **Cat Gang**, Professor von Volt gave me a gift: a digital projector and some incredible holograms!

Now I can sit on my couch and visit the most amazing places in the world! Of course, as any mouse knows, it's more fun to travel with good **friends** and **family**. And this mouse is **lucky** to have both!

YOU'RE THE INVESTIGATOR!

DID YOU FIGURE OUT THE CLUES?

1 **Why does Thea Stilton say that it doesn't add up?**
Because according to the witness's account on page 15, there are four robbers plus the huge cat. So there should be five suspects getting into the van.

2 **Look at the illustration on page 21. What does Geronimo see that is so surprising?**
The Cat Gang's van is parked in front of the bank.

3 **Do you notice something strange about the cat in Red Paparatz's photo?**
The cat has a transparent body. You can see the bars through him. He also has no shadow.

4 **Do you know how the gang of robbers makes the cat appear?**
They projected it from the van.

5 **Try to complete the sequence: What day and time will robbery #6 take place?**
Wednesday the twenty-fourth at 5 p.m. For each robbery, the robbers add a day and an hour to the previous robbery, from Monday through Wednesday.

HOW MANY QUESTIONS DID YOU ANSWER CORRECTLY?

ALL 5 CORRECT: You are a SUPER-SQUEAKY INVESTIGATOR!

FROM 2 TO 4 CORRECT: You are a SUPER INVESTIGATOR! You'll get that added squeak soon!

LESS THAN 2 CORRECT: You are a GOOD INVESTIGATOR! Keep practicing to get super-squeaky!

Farewell until the next mystery!

Geronimo Stilton

Don't miss any of my other fabumouse adventures!

#20 Surf's Up, Geronimo!

#21 The Wild, Wild West

#22 The Secret of Cacklefur Castle

A Christmas Tale

#23 Valentine's Day Disaster

#24 Field Trip to Niagara Falls

#25 The Search for Sunken Treasure

#26 The Mummy with No Name

#27 The Christmas Toy Factory

#28 Wedding Crasher

#29 Down and Out Down Under

#30 The Mouse Island Marathon

#31 The Mysterious Cheese Thief

Christmas Catastrophe

#32 Valley of the Giant Skeletons

#33 Geronimo and the Gold Medal Mystery

#34 Geronimo Stilton, Secret Agent

#35 A Very Merry Christmas

#36 Geronimo's Valentine

#37 The Race Across America

#38 A Fabumouse
School Adventure

#39 Singing
Sensation

#40 The Karate
Mouse

#41 Mighty
Mount
Kilimanjaro

#42 The Peculiar
Pumpkin Thief

#43 I'm Not a
Supermouse!

#44 The Giant
Diamond Robbery

#45 Save the
White Whale!

#46 The Haunted
Castle

#47 Run for the
Hills, Geronimo!

#48 The Mystery
in Venice

#49 The Way of
the Samurai

#50 This Hotel Is
Haunted!

#51 The Enormouse
Pearl Heist

#52 Mouse in
Space!

#53 Rumble in
the Jungle

#54 Get into
Gear, Stilton!

#55 The Golden
Statue Plot

#56 Flight of the
Red Bandit

The Hunt for the
Golden Book

ABOUT THE AUTHOR

Born in New Mouse City, Mouse Island, **GERONIMO STILTON** is Rattus Emeritus of Mousomorphic Literature and of Neo-Ratonic Comparative Philosophy. For the past twenty years, he has been running *The Rodent's Gazette*, New Mouse City's most widely read daily newspaper.

Stilton was awarded the Ratitzer Prize for his scoops on *The Curse of the Cheese Pyramid* and *The Search for Sunken Treasure*. He has also received the Andersen 2000 Prize for Personality of the Year. One of his bestsellers won the 2002 eBook Award for world's best ratlings' electronic book. His works have been published all over the globe.

In his spare time, Mr. Stilton collects antique cheese rinds and plays golf. But what he most enjoys is telling stories to his nephew Benjamin.

1. Main entrance
2. Printing presses (where the books and newspaper are printed)
3. Accounts department
4. Editorial room (where the editors, illustrators, and designers work)
5. Geronimo Stilton's office
6. Helicopter landing pad

THE RODENT'S GAZETTE

Map of New Mouse City

Map of Mouse Island

1. Big Ice Lake
2. Frozen Fur Peak
3. Slipperyslopes Glacier
4. Coldcreeps Peak
5. Ratzikistan
6. Transratania
7. Mount Vamp
8. Roastedrat Volcano
9. Brimstone Lake
10. Poopedcat Pass
11. Stinko Peak
12. Dark Forest
13. Vain Vampires Valley
14. Goose Bumps Gorge
15. The Shadow Line Pass
16. Penny Pincher Castle
17. Nature Reserve Park
18. Las Ratayas Marinas
19. Fossil Forest
20. Lake Lake
21. Lake Lakelake
22. Lake Lakelakelake
23. Cheddar Crag
24. Cannycat Castle
25. Valley of the Giant Sequoia
26. Cheddar Springs
27. Sulfurous Swamp
28. Old Reliable Geyser
29. Vole Vale
30. Ravingrat Ravine
31. Gnat Marshes
32. Munster Highlands
33. Mousehara Desert
34. Oasis of the Sweaty Camel
35. Cabbagehead Hill
36. Rattytrap Jungle
37. Rio Mosquito

Dear mouse friends,
Thanks for reading, and farewell
until the next mystery!

Geronimo Stilton